Midr
Mer
Cl

Midnight's Memoir Club

M. Hunter W.

Published by Webster-Napier, 2024.

This is a work of fiction. Similarities to real people, places, or events are entirely coincidental.

MIDNIGHT'S MEMOIR CLUB

First edition. October 20, 2024.

Copyright © 2024 M. Hunter W..

ISBN: 979-8224627127

Written by M. Hunter W..

Table of Contents

Chapter 1 1
Chapter 2 10
Chapter 3 23
Chapter 4 29
Chapter 5 37
Chapter 6 42
Chapter 7 46
Chapter 8 51
Chapter 9 56
Chapter 10 64

To My Goddaughter

Yuna

M. Hunter W.

Prologue

Sarah walked slowly up the aisle. A black ribbon tied into a bow in her long blonde hair. She held two red roses, one in each hand that dangled at the sides of her black dress. In front of her was a hazy, unfocused flood of sunlight pouring through bay windows that crowned two coffins and rows of empty red chairs sitting as silent witness'.

SARAH'S GRANDFATHER had been watching her closely and he saw that grief may soon overtake her. Gently, one night, beseeched her to start a book club, (something she had always wanted to do). In the front room, surrounded by books, he gave her some fliers, for that end, to hand out the next morning. She promised him that she would.

That next morning was a gorgeous one. The sunshine clear, the breeze was soft, and the leaves were beginning to change.

She stepped out and closed the door, her green eyes brightened by morning's rays and she tried to let the sunshine wash away some of her grief, but despite the beauty, she perceived only grey. She turned toward the road but decided that she wanted to be alone for as long as possible, so instead, she took the trails that lead down the mountain into town.

Sarah came into a clearing, one that her mother and her had rested at many times before, when they came to visit her grandfather, but though it was usually peaceful, even fairytale-like to Sarah, this time was oppressive, windy and cloudy. She caught herself there at the beginnings of a harvest storm.

The wind blew hard, fiercer than she expected. The trees groaned at her, her hair whipped around her face and eyes. She turned to run back, yet she tripped over a root on the path. Her hands came out to catch herself and the fliers slipped from her grasp and flew away from her in a torrent.

She tried at first to get them but failed even to grab a single one.

"Well Fine! I don't even care anymore!" She screamed at them. She sat down quickly and put her face into her hands and down in her knees and wept.

Where darkness fell, that's where you can find her, where loneliness dug its hole into the deep.

Chapter 1

Sarah's light brown hood waves in the cold gentle breeze of Autumn. The crunch of the leaves are under her feet as they swirl around in curiosity. The moon casts shadows, hanging just above the tree line and in front of her is a sign with two dim lights that hang on the sides of it: 'Hollister's Rare Books', her favorite bookstore. Her and her grandfather live there, up on the second story. It is a two-story building and stands in stark contrast with the woods, like a fortress against the backdrop of the king's forests. She put her Jack-O-Lantern under her arm and juggled a bag of candy, so she can open the door.

Inside, it was warm and full of light. The candles were placed in and around bookshelves and tables and she placed her pumpkin beside the old-timey cash register, sitting on a little counter, by the door. The store's filled with oddities of old things: a grandfather clock tucked in the far-left corner, lanterns and candlesticks, typewriters and old jars filled with dried herbs, and of course lots of books. Her grandfather owns this store, and if Sarah gets old enough, it will be hers.

Looking around, she saw on the mantle in front of the mirror along the right wall, a picture of her parents with her in the middle. Her eyes transfixed on it and a deep swell of pain again, began to rise and she drifted off into her mind, of the futures robbed from her and times past, and the hurtful words that...

"Are you coming daydreamer or are we divvying up the candy without you?" asked Mary Gene. The rest of the girls giggled, as they sat in the middle of the floor surrounded by books and piles of candy, and a well-placed lantern sat in the center of them. They made an area near the left wall against which had a little cabinet and a small bench then the grandfather clock. The wallpaper had vertical stripes pale blue and yellowing white and down those white stripes every so often were prints of a faded yellow lily.

"Yes, I'm coming." Sarah mumbled, as she came over and dumped the bag of candy in the circle. Mary Gene was dressed as a witch with brown curly hair to her shoulders spilling out of the pointed hat, black socks, and a raggedy black robe. She was the shortest of them all and a couple of years younger than the rest, *about thirteen*, Sarah had judged. The Lantern was tall and square. It had on it, rice paper veils, embroidered with different symbols on either side, the moon, and the sun. Two large bookshelves were to the right of them, between them and the mantle and mirrored wall.

"I just love Halloween, don't you guys?" asked Allison. Allison came dressed like an orchard farmer; a checkered tan and sky-blue dress, her meadow blonde hair in pigtail braids that reached to her shoulder blades. *She really is beautiful*, thought Sarah, her blue eyes vibrant and caring, an old soul no doubt, *she will become a teacher.*

In agreement of their love for all things Autumn and Halloween, they devoured all the chocolate they could stand.

After picking out their favorite candies and finishing the caramel apples, they set aside the piles of wrappers and each one grabbed their own book, tightening around the lantern.

They continued settling in and Allison began to shift in toward the lantern setting a book near the light, opening it to her first blank page.

Sitting between her and Mary was Ava, who came as a pirate. *Ava, a pirate,* Sarah thought, *it fit her perfectly*. She had on a black triangle hat over her straight black hair that lightly touch the tops of her shoulders, dark red dress, sleeveless, over a loose gray long sleeve shirt, and black boots. Her eyes, sharp like Egyptian eyeliner, were so dark brown they may as well be black. Sarah thought *had this been a contest, Ava would have won it*.

"OK, it's time to start I guess." Sarah announced, breaking up the murmuring. It's Allison's turn to start this meeting. She glanced at Allison who is holding her place in her book.

"Welcome, 'little women,'" her voice like honey, "To the first Halloween meeting of our book club. Since it is Halloween, I hope you all brought an excerpt from your very favorite scary book tonight. I will go fir..." Allison stopped, looking over at Mary Gene who was shaking; nearly jumping out of her own skin.

"Mary, what's wrong with you?"

"Oh, please, pleeease can I go first?" Mary Gene cried.

"No... Now we have rules Mar..."

"Please!"

"No, I said. Now..."

"But my story is so good though."

Allison turned red. "Sarah?"

"Mary, she's right. It's her turn, then Ava's, then yours." Mary Gene was about to interject again, that is until she caught sight of Ava's glare and ended up puffing out a breath of air -in great restraint.

Allison took a second to regroup. She again leaned over her book, pencil in hand.

"I will go first." She started writing. "OK. Well, tonight I'm reading from 'The Guide of the Dark Hollows'. If everyone's ready, we can start."

Allison drew close to her book while the others blew out half the candles. The room fell into a darkened orange, and the deep reds and shiny brown of the leather books melted into shadows. The globe and the statuettes and the typewriter keys shined no more. Allison began reading, slowly.

"... That night, the moon was full, and I decided I would take a shortcut through the fields to get on home. In the distance, I saw that the path fed into a dark wood, and I then realized, I've made a horrible mistake coming this way. The edge of the trees, its hard shadows, looked like gnarling teeth -ready to devour those who dared enter."

"I approached it anyway, with each step, my fear rose and fell. Me, promising myself that I would be safe, then realizing, I could not keep that promise."

Allison's eyes narrowed as she shook her head slowly staring at the lantern.

"I broke through the thicket and kneeled to one knee. Pine and cedar, that earthy scent, filled my nose, but it was pitch black in here, anything, I thought, could be lurking just there, watching me, and I would never know it." Clap! Allison smacked her hands. The girl startled back. Allison's straight face was unfazed.

"I sat for a minute with eyes keen, looking for any movements. 'What was that?,'" She jolted her body. "'Just the wind, I think.' Rustling became clear in my ears, first to the left, then to the right. Am I an animal to be preyed on? Was I like them? Would I be struck tonight?" She grabbed at her necklace.

"I felt as if an hour went by; seconds felt like minutes, minutes like hours. I mustard all the courage I could to stand –*stand*. I walked and I walked, being careful of my footing -not to make a sound, for at the snap of a twig... Trees were leaning in as if to keep watch on me."

"As I rounded the bend, I heard something ahead, and just then, a light appeared, like that of a small candle. I cautiously walked closer to it, and out of the tall bushes stepped, a woman. My eyes -they strained to see..." Allison picked up the lantern.

"I saw, though, she held a lantern, like this one... I came closer to her, and I started to speak. 'Hello miss?' I said weakly, but she didn't acknowledge me. 'I think I'm lost...', 'Are you lost too?' -nothing. She only stood there in a long white dress and long blonde hair. She was facing (almost) away from me. I started to get closer yet, when I walked, she also walked, both of us headed in the same direction."

"We were walking in silence, only hearing the gusts of wind. The wind, moving the canopies above us, sending leaves down, floating all around us. I stared at the backside of her head and the part of the face I *could* see, trying to watch for any intentions, but no expression showed. No, not any variant of movement came from her slow, gliding walk. I have never seen anything like this, I thought. I could not figure out who she is or where she was from, and I grew more and more worried when I saw that the clouds were beginning to form overhead. I wanted to ditch her, but in the distance was a black hole. Yes, at the end of this stretch was a part of the woods so thick that moonlight could not break through."

"I wondered, 'what could be in there'. And, I thought to myself, 'If there is something in there, I wanted it to get her instead of me.'"

Sarah and the rest began giggling, but with serious air, Allison shook her head, making soft shushing noises, holding the eye of each girl.

"I imagined horrors from within. My mind raced, *That sound? Did that just move? Do I see eyes?* I turned to see behind me. I turned my whole body to run, but when I faced away, I froze. I heard instantly breathing behind my ear. I felt it caress the hairs of my neck. She was standing behind me, right up against me. I stood shaking waiting for her hand to grab me, but I felt only the breaths. I didn't make a move, but I wanted so badly to run. I couldn't. It was the not knowing, my nerves ran tight in me to the point that reached a fever. I had to do something. I turned around rashly preparing to fight, and as fast as I flipped around, she was back in her place again. Every sound, I heard, like prey being stalked. Every movement, I felt, watching for an expression, waiting for a twist of her heel. The breeze was moving shadows around and playing tricks on my mind."

"Closer and closer, slowly and hesitantly, we walked to this abyss of a black hole. Until finally, we stood in front of it. I felt the cooler air rest on my skin. My knees started to shake; my legs would not move. My breath became short and shallow. Then, she... She took a step into the darkness and slowly turned toward me, her body and head fixed together like a statue. When she came full on, half of her body, the part in the darkness had melted away like wax; her white eyes stared at me through dripping skin. I turned to run. I saw her arms move up. A waxy hand grabbed my scalp -and I felt hot slime in my hair and the pain of ripping- dragging me backwards into the darkness, my feet scraping and sliding out in front of me."

"I screamed until my lungs burned. I screamed in vain, and it all went black." Allison, holding a candle, blew it out. Smoke filled the room.

"It is said to this day, if any girl walks the woods at night, alone, and she sees a lantern lit; she's doomed to be dragged into darkness and cursed till no one remembers her name." Allison laid the lantern back down and closed her book.

"OH, WOW THAT WAS A great story, Allison." Mary Gene said first.

"Yes, it was." Sarah added, "and you told it well too." Allison tried to smile.

"Really, did you guys like it?"

"It's going to be better than mine." Mary Gene cried with her fake cry.

"I loved it, Allison." Ava smiled and they all looked at Sarah.

Sarah put her arm around her and rested the side of her forehead onto hers. She could appreciate, if only for a moment. Allison smiled with a mix of pride, but her eyes remained somber.

"Thanks everyone."

8

The girls began to shift and fidget around, unwrapping candy, and shuffling books. Sarah grabbed a jar of cinnamon sticks and passed them out to each one. They raised them to their noses and smelled them. Some of them were eating toffee, and some were sucking on butterscotch, and they were having a grand old time, but Sarah caught sight of her reflection behind Ava, in the grandfather clock. It took her breath to look at it, seeing the very essence 'gloom' staring back at her. *Have they noticed this,* she glanced at each of them but they were content to be occupied. So, she put on a smile, just as the Jack-O-Lantern did behind her. *She could smile,* trying to hold it. A loud single knock hit the front door. They all stopped and stared.

Two Stories to Midnight

Chapter 2

Stunned by the noise, they stopped everything they were doing in mid-action, Mary Gene holding a sucker halfway up, Allison, with an open book, her thumb holding her page, Ava sniffing on her cinnamon stick. And Sarah twisted around to look at the door.

After a long silence, she decided to herself that she would not be scared, she could be brave... She eased to the door and looked in its side frame windows.

"What do you see?" Ava asked.

Sarah wiped the fog of her breath from it.

"Nothing." She looked back at everyone. "I'm going to open the door quickly, ok?" Ava came up beside her.

"Ok. Hold up..." She reached back for something and turned again to the door with a heavy candlestick in her hand, "...I got your back, open it."

Sarah took a deep breath and slung the door open and scanned quickly for something big but there was nothing but the fall night. With a sigh, she started to close it.

"Hey, what's that on the ground?" Mary Gene asked. She jumped up and came over. Sarah looked down. It was a black bird lying still on the mat. Mary reached to pick it up.

"Let me check if it's dead." She placed it in her hand and stroked it softly turning to come back inside. "I think it's still alive."

"Whoa, what are you doing, Mary?" Ava said quickly. Mary, startled by the brash tone, paused. "What's wrong?"

"Don't you know? It's a bad omen to have black birds in the house. And, oh, by the way it's Halloween on top of that." Ava protested.

Mary Gene kept petting the bird. "That's just superstition." She said still looking down at the bird all the while, "Look. The bird's not dead. We can just hold on to it until it wakes up and I'll let it go then, ok." Ava, not happy, closed the door behind her.

"Well, that's just fine, but when the time comes to say I told you so, you'll be hearing it." Sarah wasn't excited about it either. *Bad omens, bad luck follow me like the plague,* she thought gritting her teeth secretly.

They sat down again and began to pet the black bird and whistle and try all sorts of things to get it to wake up, but it did not wake up. They drifted into conversations about books and ghost stories, and asked Sarah about living there, in a bookstore, and she aimed to welcome this distraction as they let the time pass by -*time.*

WHEN IT *was* time to start the next book though and everyone had gotten comfortable, the bird let out a squall. It got up in front of them and jumped with a shake, looking at each girl with its own dark brown eyes, then began flying around the shelves.

After the surprise had worn off, each of the girls took their turn and tried to catch it, but it just flew up high, on the shelves and the beams not letting anyone get close, while they took care trying not to disturb the candles or the antiques. Yet still they jarred the locked cabinet near the café entrance -between the front door and the left wall- and it was dark as night through the café to the kitchen's archway.

Finally, Sarah had enough. She grabbed the homemade broom that Mary Gene had brought and started swiping at it. At one point it almost went outside, but at the last second turned to its left, over the counter, midways down the wall and landed on the low mantle in front of the mirror. Sarah tiptoed toward it, head on. The bird looked directly at her, it gave a squall and *purposely*, thought Sarah, used its beak to topple a picture of her and her parents to the ground to break it -right down the center. Sarah's face turned red, and she came at the bird fast and hard. It must have sensed the sudden change, as this time it darted straight out into the windy night. The door shut and Sarah immediately went to picking up the glass, mumbling something under her breath and for a short minute was oblivious to anyone else in the room.

"Ok. Go ahead and say it, Ava." Mary held her head down. Ava looked confused.

"Say what?" Mary Gene's eyes glanced skeptically.

"That you told me so."

"Oh, Noo, Mary. You know. That was the omen part not the bad luck part." She gave Sarah a quick glance and looked at Mary. "I had fun chasing that bird anyhow. Aside from the end."

After a minute of straightening things back around, Allison pointed behind Sarah who just picked up the last of the glass.

"What's in the cabinet, Sarah?"

Sarah looked by the threshold of the café at the three-foot-tall cabinet with glass doors and an old lock holding it shut.

"That. It's books and keepsakes that my grandpa kept, from our family members that have passed away... He has rare books in there too." They all leaned in for a closer look. It had old pictures and books in there, but up on the top shelf something caught everyone's eye. A hardcover case of dark faded green had been opened when they hit the cabinet. Inside, folded to its curve, was a weathered picture of Sarah's grandmother and her 'young' mother wearing an emerald necklace, the same one that was spilling out the side of the faded green case.

Sarah rushed to the cash register and opened it. Digging hurriedly through it, she came back with a key.

She held the picture up in the candlelight and aligned the necklace up to it, her back was still turned to the others for that moment, and just before they could gather close to her, the picture ignited in a flash of a green flame. Sarah dropped it and it landed on the hardwood floor. She stomped on it quickly. Her foot backed off, and she, beside herself now, stared only at ash.

"What happened?" Mary Gene asked in alarm, "Did you hold it to close to the candle?"

"Yes, I must have." She said absently. Allison came up beside her and rested her hand on her shoulder.

"I'm sorry that happened." Sarah remained looking at the floor. Allison continued to gaze at her, and the others came up close around her. Sarah soon came back to herself; she didn't let herself tear up.

"It's all right, thanks you all," She straightened herself up again, "Let's look at this necklace." She managed a convincing smile.

"THAT'S THE MOST BEAUTIFUL thing I've ever seen." Sarah said seemingly to herself. She couldn't take her eyes off it; she could desire. Allison's eyes followed the gold chain and setting.

"It's gorgeous. I wonder what it's worth?"

"Your SOUL!" Ava clamped on Allison's ribs. Allison jumped and screamed.

"Ava! That's not funny!", but she couldn't hear her because she was laughing too hard.

Sarah put on the necklace. "Well, how about we get on to our next story?", she said glancing at the clock. Ava could barely contain her amusement.

"Ok, ok, sorry Alli."

They all made their way back to the floor and Allison, still shaking off her jolt, opened her book and wrote in it. Ava then grabbed her book, watching until everyone was ready and after everyone settled in, she began...

"This is called 'Guardians of Midnight Island.'"

"...THE WAVES THREATENED to overtake us. The thunder clasped and the winds took on a gale. I had threatened to be washed overboard but I held on for dear, dear life. Cutting through the tops of waves I looked toward the island, but the night was so dark, and the storm so thick that it only showed when the lightning struck. Black jagged cursed thing it was too!"

"We rowed hard for the beach. Five souls onboard including our captain. I tucked my collar under my ears and the waves relentlessly crashed over us. I leaned my head into the driving rain. *Just think of the treasure*, I mouthed. *All those riches*.

"Row...Row...Row..." cried the captain. My arms burned. I twisted my body and leaned forward and backward, struggling to find different parts of muscles to work.

"We're nearly there. Row!" Ordered the captain over the wind. In unison, we rowed nearing the island's surf.

"Mind those rocks!" Yelled my captain. "Swing port...Head for the clearing!" We pulled with everything we had, and the surf was bound and determined to throw us to the rocks.

"Row! Get clear those rocks now or she'll take us under!" A large swell toppled over us, and I don't know how but, *nearly*, we missed the rocks at the edge of the clearing. The sea spit us out and flipped us onto the beach. Me, on my back, laid there as the rain pelted my face. I was glad to be alive; unable to lift my arms.

"Breaks over lads." The captain finally said. "Bring that boat up and get me my lamp." We dragged the boat on shore, and I untethered the leather bag. The men held the boat up enough for me to light the oil lamp and the strips of oil-soaked clothes we used for our torches.

"Captain, which way are we headed? We stand on the north side of the island." He studied his map, to which, I noticed the corner had been torn with the word 'Beware the ...'

"'What happened here captain? Where's the corner?'"

"'That's still in the dead man's hand.' He said matter-of-factly. 'Spread out men. You're looking for the mouth of a cave a hundred paces due south.'"

"The rain was letting up and the thunder moved farther and farther into the distance. The wind though, the cursed wind, showed no sign of relenting.'

"We kept out lines as we spread out through the trees and brush. I took up position more toward the rear. Our torches whipped in the winds, the lightening illuminated the shadows, and the trees danced but were holding strong. About fifty paces in through, one of the men hollered from my left. 'Keep your eyes! I think there's something in the shadows. I could swear to it.'"

"'I think the night's playing tricks on ya.' Another said."

"'I'm telling you; I saw something. If it ain't nothing, what does it hurt to watch. But you have it your way then.'"

"We walked on and I decided, if there is something out there, I wanted to know. So, for every three paces I spun around to see behind me."

"'Hey watch it!' This time from the right of me. 'I don't think he's mistaken, captain, I believe I saw something lurking over there.'"

"'Tighten up then,' Our captain ordered. 'Get closer and draw your arms.' I looked heavy into the trees and drew my dagger. The rest pulled their swords and the captain, his flintlock with a mounted blade on the end."

"'I don't care what's out there.' He hollered, 'We've come this far and we're going all the way. Now don't ya turn yellow on me.'"

"We carried on toward the mark, the men darting their heads left, right, and back again. The lightening and torches flickering shadows, dancing the demons all around us. I gripped tight on my dagger's handle."

"'There she is, mates.' The captain cried out, 'Get the lights up here.' In front of us loomed a jagged mouth of a cave and vines ran up its triangled edges. I walked in first and I felt pure relief to be in, out of the wind. As more light flooded in the cave, what struck me was the height and the glisten of the ceiling and the walls. In the center of the ceiling was a large hole, and the clouds whipped by. Under its hole was the object of our efforts, a large wood and iron chest sitting on an unhewed rock. *We're going to be rich*, I thought to myself."

"One of our biggest men grabbed the biggest rock he could manage and squared himself in front of the lock. He looked to the captain."

"'Do it.' Our captain ordered. The rock came down with a smash, bits of rock and metal went flying into the dark corners of the cave."

"The captain cracked open the lid and we leaned in, but something caught our attention -silence. The wind, which had been so persistent, went stone cold dead. I went to look up through the hole, but my eyes didn't make it there, for just at the edge of our light, in the dark of the cave I saw three sets of paws, black and sharp."

"'Captain, look out!' I pointed. Weapons went up. I backed off a pace or two and instinctively looked up toward the hole. There sat two more, two black wolf-like creatures staring down at us; shrouded by smokey-fur that whipped close around to their bodies."

"I couldn't make sense of what I was seeing when all-a-sudden the two from up-top jumped down opposite the chest, as noiseless as death itself. I turned to run, but when I turned, I was face to face with another one. Out of pure reflex, I slashed at its head with all my might, my dagger went through it as if it were made of water. It jumped I threw myself to the left. I landed on my side in great pain by a sharp rock... It started toward me when a shot rang out, and I took my opportunity to run."

"When I reached the opening, I looked back to see if the rest were still with me and I could tell they were, so I ran headlong for the beach."

"Arriving at the beach, I was out of breath. 'What the hell was that?' I cried. We scurried to get the boat to the surf, when someone hollered that we were missing one, but before anyone could respond, a loud cry echoed through the trees."

"'Captain, this has to do with that gold,' I said, 'Did you swipe any of it? I can try to save his life.' He reached into his pocket and pulled out gold coins and gemstones. Quickly, I put them into my leather pouch and ran back for the cave."

"As the trees ripped by me, I could see one of the beings keeping pace with me, running parallel to me, only separated by vegetation. Fear pushed me faster than I thought capable. Another shadow came in from my left-front to intercept me. Just before colliding, I dove and rolled hard but popped up like a spring."

"I ran so hard into the cave, I figured if anything did grab me, my momentum alone would break me free. Without thinking, I lifted the chest's lid and threw the bag in. I hollered out for the lost but heard nothing. Not wasting any time, I dashed back out into the night. I didn't see any of the wolves, but I wasn't stopping to contemplate it either. I hollered again. This time I heard a faint yelp over to the east, in the brush."

"He lay bloodied, but alive. Half his scalp clawed nearly from his head; blood drenched his shirt. I helped him up and we went to run, only, we were surrounded. I tried to leap over one, but I fell in a mess of fur and teeth and blood, and flesh and eyes -devilish red eyes… but, I refuse to scream."

Mary's eyes stood wide open.

"Whoa, that was a wild ride."
"Yeah, that'll be my favorite story of the night." Allison said. Ava grinned with satisfaction.
"I thought you would like that, Alli.'"
"Is that why you dressed as a pirate?" Sarah asked in awe. Ava nodded. "Yes. It adds a little extra to the story, don't you think?"
"Yeah…" Sarah became impressed by Ava's instincts. "That's so cool, I love it." Ava glowed in the praise of her friends, but it didn't last too long.

ALLISON RAISED QUICKLY from her seat. "Hey. Look out there." She pointed toward the door's windows. Sarah turned and saw through them what looked like hundreds of bats or black birds flying by in a flurry. She jumped up; they all did, and Sarah positioned herself to see out the bay windows of the café.

A rushing wind whistled around the house so threatening that Sarah thought it might bring the walls in around them. Mary Gene took a deep breath. "What's going on Sarah?"
"I'll check it out." She replied without looking back.

She cracked the door open with her right hand up, as if carrying a shield. The wind pushed the door from her hand and slammed it into the counter. Stepping out, her eyes looked off to the right. In the distance a great storm had been brewing this whole time.

"It's just leaves." She said, her blonde hair whipping wildly. "It's really windy out here though." Ava grinned slyly. "Is it a gale?" Sarah still staring in the distance.

"Yeah, Ava, actually it is." At that, Ava and Mary Gene came out and saw the huge dark clouds. They towered to the stars, in the distance, and the lightening, internal and dark blood red amplified their terror.

"This is going to be bad." Proclaimed Ava. Sarah felt that something wasn't quite going right in the world. She could *see* fates hand.

"Mmm...Who wants some hot chocolate?" Sarah asked quickly. Mary Gene grabbed her by the hand. "Yes, please." She dragged Sarah in, and they huddled their way through the café and into the doorless kitchen.

The kitchen has a gorgeous wooden island in the center and white counters over natural wood shelves and cabinets -standing against the outer wall. On top of the counter sat brown and red clay jars of spices and sugar, honey and cocoa, flour and coffee.

Sarah grabbed one of the clay jars from the middle and scooped from it, cocoa, into five white cups. Ava filled the tea pot with water and lit the stove. Allison grabbed the marshmallows and scooped the honey and Mary Gene did a jig in front of the island, having no plans to stop until her cup 'be filled with drink'. There were laughs and smiles all around, the air filling with comfort. Yet subtly, when not in immediate action, Sarah began to take deep breaths and placed her hand on the counter focusing out the window, out at the coming storm behind her reflection. She could hide it.

22

One Story to Midnight

Chapter 3

Ava's amusement didn't last.

"You're crowding me, Mary." She snapped. Mary Gene, unfazed, danced a few paces toward Sarah, who took notice. Ava took off the teapot after a few whistles. "Ok, get your cups ready." Mary Gene jumped to the head of the line and Ava poured each cup in turn.

Sarah took a knife from the counter, slowly twisting it in her hand. She turn to the island and cut each one a slice of pumpkin pie that she saved just for tonight. The room lifted with the scents of cocoa and honey and spices, and just for a little while, the house fell quiet.

ONCE ALL WERE DONE, Allison had put her cup down last. "It's starting to get late ladies, let's get Mary Gene's story over with." Mary's face instantly turned red.

"Whyy do you have to say it like that?" Mary Gene cried. This time it was very nearly a real cry, that caught Allison off guard.

"I didn't mean anything by it." Allison said seeing her error, she came up beside Mary Gene, who's eyes held back buckets of water, and put her arm around her. "I didn't mean anything by it Mary... You know we save the best for last." She said very softly.

She made herself low. "It's the one we'll dream about tonight, you know." She, with bright blue eyes, smiled. *It seemed to work,* Sarah thought, as Mary Gene's eyes smiled, a very genuine smile. So, they herded through the dark café back into the front room.

After settling back in their places, Allison continued.

"Ok, for our next, *and probably best*, story of the night, it's Mary Gene's turn... Ok Mary, what's the name of your book?"

"The Curious and the Cursed"

She wrote in her book. "Ok, whenever you're ready Mar..."

"The Curious and the Cursed" Mary started and then cleared her throat.

"...'I don't care what they say anymore.' She said pacing in her room alone. 'She needs my help. I just know she does.' She looked across the way from her second story window, passed the bridge and the church to the old mansion on the hill surrounded by run down iron fences and twisted leafless trees and the high dead grass."

"'I have to go there.' Her face showed her turmoil. She tied her bed sheets into knots and tied them to the bed post, opened her window, and climbed to the cobblestone streets below."

"The night was foggy, and the sea sent a breeze that chilled her to the bone. She clinched up her robe and walked toward the bridge, the light of the lamps could hardly reach below their posts to the stone walls."

"When she passed in front of the church, the bell rang out, cutting through the silence of the town and shaking her to her core -had she been found out. She, then, quickened her pace. At the iron gate of the old mansion, she paused and looked around.

She grasped the iron, and with more force than she thought she'd need, she managed to swing the gate open. She found herself confused by this."

"Briskly, she went through the untamed yard and slung the front door open without hesitation. The foyer was large, pale light trickled in the front windows from the town below, and dust and cobwebs were its decoration. It was abandoned, yet furnished, as if who ever lived here had long since been gone. There were grand stairs to the left side that went up to the walk above. From the foyer looking over the hand railing, were three doors tightly shut, part of a long hallway."

"She made her way upstairs as casually and intentionally as if she were calling on a friend. Down the hall to the left was pitch black, all the doors shut, but to the right, at the end of the hall, a door cracked open. She rushed to the door but opened it slowly. Inside was a large library. Shelves were everywhere, cover in dust and rundown. A wall of windows looked out to sea. Some of the panes were cracked; some were gone but all were covered in dust. She heard a creaking in toward the back."

"She mazed her way toward its direction. The creak was rhythmic -back and forth, back and forth. She came to the last shelf between her and the sound. She eased her head around the corner and to her horror, a woman hanged from the beam above her. Her skin gray and cracked; her hair dried out like black moss. It hung there, wearing a night gown, and her feet swings back and forth. 'I am mad!' She proclaimed looking up at it. Suddenly, the rope snapped, and the body fell to the hard, wood floor at her feet. She looked at it stunned, lying there, and for a moment, she contemplated getting closer but as she came to the threshold of tension while reaching out, the body moved.

A jerk of its shoulder at first. Then all at once it stood straight up. The body rocked, softly and slowly, while turning itself around till it was full on her, facing her. When she looked upon it, she saw holes where eyes had once been."

"It cried loudly, a blood curdling cry. 'YOU!', 'Now... Now you will have my curse.' At that, the body dropped dead again, and the skin waxed over into petrification. In that very instant, as she turned to run, a light had left her body through her eyes and she saw as this light, her soul, flew from her and faded out through the ceiling. If terror itself could be purified and injected. It was injected into her. Complete and total hopelessness replaced her soul. Every *minute* form of 'identity' she thought she could hold onto, had gone from her. She became hollow. To be 'mad' would have been a step up from this; to be insane -a gift."

"She ran from there, chasing something. Something she could never get back. She ran. She was looking for her life. She ran back into her room and to her bed, hoping she could get some comfort but only the feeling of damnation. Her mind stayed in constant panic. It kept her awake the whole night. Her body shook in terror. She could remember no joy. In her own hell, she couldn't think of even one happy thought. If one had come close it was overwhelmed by how meaningless it all was and any future was all meaningless."

"She couldn't sleep all the following day. When she closed her eyes to sleep and it was almost upon her, a terrible vision would wake her. A friend yelling at her and slapping the back of her head or a solitary flower would grow in a black setting and immediately die. The physical panic never let up. It's as if she was stuck in the moment of one's death, her death, and it stayed there. It lingered."

"Night had fallen again. She knew she could live like this no more, so she paced and paced, trying to find distraction. It caught the attention of one of the servants who came up to check on her."

"'Are you all right, miss?' She asked."

"'I'm fine.' She lied, not looking directly at her. Her expression and the inability to be still gave her away. She noticed the concern on the servant's face and when she left, she knew that she'd go directly to the doctor; the door locked."

"This compounded her panic to its heightened-most. A horrifying thought came to her. 'When they lock me up, I'll have to live like this forever.' That thought was the final straw, and she pulled the sheets back out the window into the night. Rushing to the bridge, she stood on the stone sides. 'This is the only way.' A voice repeated it. 'This is the only way.' She leaned forward, and passed the point of balance, cutting a silhouette into the foggy night -just beyond the lights of the stone wall bridge."

"WOW... I DID NOT EXPECT that kind of story from someone your age." Sarah said, "That was really beautiful" Ava looked concerned.

"Yeah, Mary... That was a bit too intense." Ava replied and held Mary with a critical look.

Mary Gene's face began a deep frown.

"I'm only a couple years younger than you all." She said. The tension between them started to fill the room.

"Please. Let's drop that, ok?" Allison's gaze landed on Ava.

Ava put her hands up in surrender.

"Ok with me."

Mary Gene automatically beamed with a big smile, which she shifted to Ava, who just rolled her eyes.

"That was a great story." Sarah said, seemingly to herself. She looked up and she smiled.

"Oh, yeah, Mary. It was..." Allison snuck a glance at Sarah who stared absently again at the floor, "...intense."

"Right. It was super creepy." Ava said quickly. The way one does to keep a bad essence out of the room.

"Oh, you did so well." Allison said with a hug, "Do you want me to get you some more hot chocolate?"

"Yes, please." ...Allison left to the kitchen.

Chapter 4

Sarah, who had become increasingly more detached throughout the night, was inspecting her necklace absently. Without a word, she got up and went behind the front counter, where the Jack-O-Lantern sat, kneeling behind it, moving things around, she pulled out a jar of sucker-straws, the homemade type.

Her and Allison came back to their spots in the floor together at the same time.

Allison gave the cup of cocoa to Mary Gene as she sat, but all their eyes were on Sarah and her jar of suckers. It was five minutes to midnight.

Sarah took out the only black sucker, looking intently on it. She then realized that she was at the center of attention, so she held the open mouth of the jar toward Mary. Mary looked at it *oddly* -an air of grave sadness and looked up again at Sarah.

"I would like the black one... If you don't mind?" Mary said. Sarah winced involuntarily.

"No. I'm sorry Mary, but I saved this one for Myself tonight."

Again, a gesture of the jar. Mary reached in and grabbed a blue straw and looked into Sarah's eyes and put it in her mouth.

Sarah swung the jar over the lantern to Ava. Ava began to reach in but stopped close to the edge of it -she had an air of seriousness, even more so. "I really do love black suckers, won't you part with it for me?" Sarah matched the expression of Ava.

"No. I'm sorry." Ava's stare lasted a little longer, but finally she looked back into the jar again.

"Ok." She said and reached in to get a red one.

Sarah began to feel... She turned the jar one last time to Allison. Allison did not reach for a sucker.

"I'd like the black sucker please."

Sarah's arm began to shake at the jar. She first looked confused, but quick looks of fear and of anger flashed in her eyes -*almost* imperceptibly. In response to Allison's statement, she simply shook her head ever-slightly. Allison reached up and in and grabbed a yellow sucker.

Her guests were eating their sucker-straws in silence, but Sarah stared at hers and stared and she wasn't smiling.

"Hey, daydreamer... If you don't want to eat it, you can throw it in the trash. That'll be fair to all of us." She gave a quick smile. The others nodded in agreement.

Sarah breathed and looking again at her sucker. She couldn't... She put the sucker in her mouth, bit on it and swallowed it.

At that very moment, a soft bell rang from the grandfather clock -midnight. Three knocks came from the front door.

A SHARP SILENCE ENTERED the room with the last one. Their cares fell to dust. Eyes intently held on the oak barrier between these girls and the fear of the known and of the unknown. Sarah looked through the little windows but only saw (as far as she could) the passing of leaves and the black shadows across the street, held back by moonlit trees.

She thought maybe, it was a black bird again, or, it was another girl to join her club, at midnight; just as Allison did the last weekend and Ava the weekend prior and Mary Gene, that first.

Her confidence began to waver though, as the tips of her fingers brushed the doorknob. She stared at her hand -shaking. She felt a hand rest on her shoulder.

Looking out the corner of her eye she knew that Ava was there, and she smiled when she saw that Ava held that brass candlestick in her hand. With a deep breath, the door was flung open; a candlestick was raised high up and stayed. Outside stood a girl whose face is shrouded by a dark hood and there is a book, held up in front of her, for use of a shield. When the initial shock was worn over, everyone lowered their guards and weapons.

They stood in silence. Sarah moved aside and with a gesture of her hand to invite the stranger in. She noticed the look Ava flashed for a split second; one of those things that burns in the memory. Mary Gene kept her distance when the new girl walked through the door. Allison came closer to Sarah. This girl stood in the center of the loosely formed circle of friends and removed her hood. Her hair was dark brown. The lights flickered at the sudden change of air from the shutting door.

No-one spoke as this girl's eyes move over each one of them, she landed on Sarah with an expression of expectation, one of introductions. Sarah's fingers pointed at her chest, "My names' Sarah". She glanced down at her book, "Have you come for the book club?" The girl looking at Sarah, with dark brown eyes, handed her a damaged flier.

"Yes. If you don't mind?" Sarah took the flier and laid it on the little counter.

"No, I don't mind at all. What's your name?"

"My name is Mara."

"This is Allison, Mary Gene, and Ava. Come with me and sit here beside me." Sarah made room beside her, and they sat down together. The other girls, who had not spoken yet, slowly sat down in their places. Each looking, staring at the two of them together. Sarah hardly noticed the change in the room as she made small talk with Mara.

Sarah folded up her own book and pushed it aside. "Alright, since I was going to go next, I'll give my spot to you." Sarah made a gesture to her book. "That's really old looking, how old is it?"

With admiring eyes, Mara rubbed its surface.

"It's centuries old." Sarah absently smiled at the book and unnoticed by her, each of the three girls, sitting on their pillows had lowered their heads and looked down at the ground in front of them, but Sarah did finally become concerned when Mara opened her book because she then realized that the new girl's whole body was pointed toward her only and that none of her friends had spoken since she came in. Her eyes locked in on the top of Mara's head as she was reading very softly, at first. Her reading seemed almost chanting. She, looking up, became louder, louder and louder.

Heaviness fell on Sarah's mind and body. In the room, the candles began flickering, going dim. The voice seemed to surround the whole room and enveloped her by the aid of a darkening cloud, until just before total darkness and loud as ever, she saw only the slightest rim light touching her friends' figures.

33

IN TOTAL DARKNESS, she had felt herself void, as if no weight were on skin or bones or even organs. Sarah was floating and her body was moving forward. The air around her felt thin. No sound was heard. She could smell…moisture. She tried to move -her hands and arms, legs and feet could flail about, but no progress was made in her directions.

She screamed but no sound came out. Fear took her and in a psychotic panic, she screamed and thrashed about with not so much as a whisper being sounded. Her throat burned to coughing and tears fell down her cheeks. She reached up and wiped them off. She could feel.

A small thing can give hope, and for Sarah, that came in the form of a distant light. She stopped moving and screaming, so in case that, by some bazar action, it would disappear from her.

Little by little, she moved, but the light, imperceptibly at first, had grown all the while. So, she moved bigger and wider and faster circles, until it very much mimicked swimming. She was close enough now to see it –a campfire.

Soon, the heat warmed her. Her eyes filled with its amber. All at once her elbows and knees stopped floating and found solid ground as she crawled another few paces and sat at the fire, hugging her knees. That hopeful warmth rushed over her. She sat looking over tops of trees into the vast open sky crowded by stars of every hue and brilliant colors and never the one, the same as another. She sat awestruck. "I've never seen this many stars." she said aloud, still looking.

"It's really beautiful, isn't it?"

Sarah's skin crawled in an instant, her heart skipped, and before she could utter "who's there" Mary Gene stepped out of the shadowy bushes. Her hands lay clasped together in front of her holding her hat.

"Mary Gene!" Sarah cried and ran up to embrace her. Mary tried to say something, but her face was buried in Sarah's vest.

Sarah pulled her away. "Where are we, what is this place Mary, what happened?"

She looked at her and saw tears begin to well up.

"I'm so sorry, Sarah. There's nothing we could've done to stop it, or we'd be punished, please! Won't you forgive us?", at that she again buried her face in shame. Sarah looked down at her bewildered. She laced her fingers through her hair, her eyes softened.

"I accept your apology... for whatever you've done." She tried to console her.

Her tears began anew, though. Sarah looked up at the treetops and held Mary close. There was a hint of the moon coming up -a remnant glow just behind the subtle slopes at her left.

"If your calm enough, please, tell me what's happening?"

"Mary Gene." Mary pulled her head out and took a step back.

"Okay. I will."

Sarah managed a smile. Mary took hold of her hands. "That girl that you let in, she's pure evil and she tortures us, and this island is her playground. When she finds a girl so broken..." Mary's voice cracked. "That they would consider doing what you did..." Sarah blushed quickly looking down and away. "So, it's always you, Ava, and Allison?" She asked.

"Yes… and Kailey." They stood by a fire, but they trembled.

"When this happens and has happened." Mary continued, "We are here to witness and to…" Her voice trailed again as she shook. Sarah grabbed Mary's shoulders firmly. The same way her mother had done when she couldn't stop crying.

"To what Mary!? Brought here to what?!"

"To suffer!" Mary Gene cried and shook in her place. "You'll watch each of us hurt and killed, and we'll never know what happens to you."

Sarah stood stunned, not wanting to, but having to believe it as she looked around and considered all that is happening and where she now stood. She felt the heat on her skin and smelled the burnt hickory smoke of the campfire. She knew, this was real. She opened her mouth to say something, but the air suddenly changed.

"We have to start." Mary Gene said. While she was still speaking, just to Sarah's left in the direction of the rising moon, tiny white-hot lights illuminated on short, thin iron black poles, and the light shined with an orange hue. They staggered on either side of the well-worn trail. Mary's hand clasped Her's and they began walking up the path.

Over the crest of that small slope a long orangish trail led for a good length, beside it the wooded left, and the right side was a field of all kinds of low bushes and plants and briers growing wild that went over slopes and hills and valleys to another far-off wood. The moon made it all surprisingly bright, and they walked together, hand in hand.

SARAH LOOKED AROUND, evaluating, and weighing everything in her mind.

"So.., what would happen if I tried and ran?" She finally asked Mary Gene. Mary's grip tightened up a bit.

"Try it and you'll see." They stopped there and Sarah investigated the woods to their left. Mary came close to her as she neared the first of the trees.

"Don't let go of my hand Sarah." Mary's grip moved to be more secure, around her wrist. Sarah stepped in. Immediately, a black thick fog came in from the deep parts of the woods and surrounded her, the trees, and the plants alike. Leaving only the glistens of the glowing path. Mary's hand rose up in the black fog. She leaned back and pulled hard. Sarah flew down on top of her and the void slithered soundlessly into the shadows it had once come.

"I was in that terrible void again." She said getting up and straightening down her clothes.

"I call it the black curtain." Mary replied.

"We can't stop too long." Mary said again after a few more steps. "The last girl was so unhinged she tried to run off three times and when she came back the third time, she had gone completely mad."

"That's awful, what happened to her?"

Mary stopped. "She jumped off the first cliff she came to, but when I went to the edge and looked over, I never saw her body... we didn't get tormented that time."

Chapter 5

They walked a while in silence and coming over the crest of another small hill, to Sarah's great surprise, she saw a massive sea that came from the darkest edge of the world; The moon shined, and its reflection seemed like a mural in the waves, and the sea disappeared under the edge of the cliffs in front of them.

On the top of this cliff was a large clearing that opened-up to the right and a single run-down cabin stood off. It's boards near the roof were falling, the interior was dark as a hole and the black birds were sitting on the roof mind their own. Mary grabbed Sarah's right arm trembling and tightened around her wrist.

"This is where it starts for me." Sarah heard the fear in her voice. Mary took a deep breath and a very shaky sigh.

Sarah's eyes filled with concern looking at her friend who was so obviously scared to death, not taking her eyes off the cabin.

"What usually happens?"

"There's an old nasty woman and she traps me and burns me alive." The setting is always different, but the end is always the same." Sarah looked behind her as if to find an escape. She saw that the trail and the fields and woods began to dim, like the moon's light couldn't quite reach it.

She looked again at the cabin. "Okay... let's go. Stay behind me." Which Mary was only too glad to do.

The soft sounds of the sea's shore now reached up to them, they were close enough to smell the salt mixed in with the rotting musk of the cabin.

Sarah walked near the side door and reached down, keeping her eyes focused inside the windows of it when she caught sight, in reflection, of a green glow just under the clasp of her light brown hood. She took her hand back and untucked her necklace.

"Mary Gene, look! My necklace." She whispers. Mary craned her head around from behind. The green showed bright in their eyes.

"I've never seen anything like that here, but Ava and Allison told me they often see a red glow when they get hunted." Mary was getting excited and almost started the jig she had done in the kitchen of the bookstore.

"I had a brilliant thought."

"What is it?"

"What if that could be a weapon here, like some kind of power. Oh God, we could be saved." She tried to control her breathing.

Sarah stood, fiddling at it...confused. "We have to try, I guess."

"Trust me Sarah, we need as much hope as we can get."

Sarah had the weird advantage of not knowing what's going on and stared down at her emerald once again.

"But how can I use it as a weapon?"

Mary was bouncing after looking behind them. "I don't know use it like a num-chuk or something, but we need to go in?"

Sarah unclasped the necklace and opened the door. Once in, they looked around slowly, huddled. Sarah looked back at the black curtain – it stopped on the hill they had once been. They creeped in, and to their left was a run-down dining area, covered in cobwebs and the film of greyish blue hue of dust and moonlight, much like the whole of the island. A rotting table and chairs sat in the center and a draft of salty sea air came in through unseen cracks of windows and walls.

They stood in a kitchen of the same condition with a cast iron stove, near the shadows in the corner beside flaking cabinets. To the right was a hallway which they walked down. The sounds of the shoreline were replaced by creaks of dry floorboards. Slowly, they made it halfway down the darkened hall, windows on the right, doors on the left.

A violent sound popped behind them -Sarah's heart jumped to her throat again.

"Jesus!" Sarah cried, flipping around.

The door had snapped from its top hinge and dust swirled into the shadows. The door now stood skewed. Sarah's neck thumped from its sides until her adrenaline came back down. Mary's nails released from the skin of Sarah's arms. They both turned again down the hall. Mary in front, slowly made her way to the opened door at the far end. Her hand reached the edge; with her fingertips she pushed the door open, it slowly growled, but just then something pushed Sarah violently aside, her right shoulder, neck, and elbow crashed through the window. A boney, grey hand grabbed the scruff of Mary's collar and jerked her backward toward the kitchen.

Sarah pulled herself back into the house and felt a sharp pain in between her neck and shoulder. She looked back toward the kitchen which was now lit up in yellow glow. Sarah felt sick and dizzy and heard muffled pleading. She lifted her hand up to her neck and she felt something hard and jagged sticking out of her skin. Glass – she pulled on it and it rubbed up the sides of flesh, skin, and muscle. The glass slid painfully out of her body. She saw a white light and puked.

Sarah staggered to the kitchen coming face to face with a hollowed corpse woman with dead dross hair, leathery grey skin, and empty eye sockets. It seemed everything had been paused -except for Mary's squirming- just for her.

Mary wasn't pleading anymore. The witch held her up by the throat with one hand and the other held an old-style broom, with the round bristles – pointed at Sarah's face. She froze. Mary's face started to change color, but Sarah remembered her necklace. She made the slightest move of it to which the corpse thrusted the broom at Sarah's chest.

It felt as though a huge foot had knocked her back. She saw her feet in the air and then a doorframe and then a whole cabin before sliding in grass on her back. The witch gave a swipe of the broom, and the door tried to slam shut at its skewed angle. Through the windows of the door, she saw Mary Gene's feet and arms thrashing wildly, her body being held up at a high angle.

The dead witch set down her broom and began to slap Mary's face until Mary's witch hat fell off her head. Her hair whipped around wildly at each hit, and blood spilled from her nose. Sarah jumped up, her skin red hot.

"Oh, Hell No!" Her voice came from deep. The witch was violently stuffing Mary into the oven, but in a huffing - seething - breathing bellow, Sarah ran hard at the door -jumped in a blind rage- her elbows and knees slammed wood and glass. Glass shattered and the door splintered; just as the crusty grey fingertips touched the broom handle, a bright green streak came down fast from over Sarah's shoulder, and it came down hard. Two bodies hit cabinets, then two bodies fell to the floor. Sarah landed on her hind-end; a severed head rolled between her legs.

Mary clamored out of the oven, standing behind her, covered in soot and wiping away the tears and blood, she was struggling to breath; afraid to touch her friend while her body still bellowed in rage.

After the red heat washed from her eyes Sarah got up and kicked the head away from her as Mary fitted again her witch's hat.

Wrapped in each other's arms whilst glass cracked under their feet, they left the cabin.

SARAH BEGAN SHIVERING and quit moving. Holding her hands to her face. She started crying, her shoulders shook in between bouts of dry heaves. Mary pulled in closer, hugging her tightly, and this time it was her who would give comforts and pets to someone.

Chapter 6

They could see the cliff ahead, the black curtain to their right, and the cliffs that went down to the shores on their left. They were stuck going straight to that high jagged cliff.

They closed in on the base at the shadows, where it over-hanged. The moon showed how unruly and sharp the rocks protruded from its side. Sarah's necklace began glowing, her breath shallowed, and her fist tightened around the emerald.

"Mary! Sarah! Come over here." They heard a voice whispering. Mary ran into the dark overhang. Sarah bent over straining her eyes.

"Allison, is that you?"

"Yes, get under here, quick." Allison whispered. They shined in the glow of the emerald. Allison gave a nervous glance up.

"How did you make it past your witch, Mary?"

"Oh, you won't believe this. Sarah has a secret weapon! It's that necklace, and she cut the witch's head clean off." Allison stared at it curiously.

"Why do we have to whisper?" Sarah asked.

"She's above us. She likes to kick loose stones down on my head to try and kill me."

"Who is she?"

"She? She's the woman from my story, didn't Mary tell you?"

"No... I mean only that I have to watch you get tortured and killed in front of me."

"That's right. She's...She is the woman from my story." They jumped when a stone fell near their feet.

"We have allowances on Halloween you see, and one of those is that she lets us tell any story we want as long as it won't directly warn her prey...That's you." Sarah was taken back, being called prey.

"Me? Why..."

"There's no more time Sarah, look! The black fog is coming."

Sarah, Mary, and Allison began climbing. Sarah was struck with an idea. "Spread out guys, ok. Let's reach the top at the same time, try and confuse her, then I will swing my necklace at her, ok."

Each one gave a nod. Allison climbed toward her left and Mary to her right.

The climb was not an easy one and Sarah wanted badly to rub on her neck. She had yet to see the woman, but her hands were getting fatigued; her legs were in burning pain and she tried desperately to control her fear -not looking down. All the while getting higher, a tunnel of wind from the lower cliffs whipped over the tops and pushed against their sides clinging their clothes against their bodies.

Nearing the top, Allison slipped off one of her holds. She made a gasp and a yelp and that was enough. She regained her grip immediately, and Sarah saw just above her, the woman in white gliding to the edge of the cliff, her lantern held out. It looked down, her head only slightly bent forward at the neck.

Her feet weren't seen for her long sweeping dress, and from it came a stone the size of two fist held together.

"Watch it!" Sarah yelled.

Allison moved just as the stone came near her left hand.

"Hey!" Mary cried out. Sarah watched as the woman went past her with unnatural speed and stepped on Mary's hand. Mary let out a scream more from terror than from pain. She, with presence of mind, shoved her hand into a clevis just as the lady in white stepped on her other. Again, she cried out.

Sarah's fist tightened around the necklace chain, and she steadied herself on a tiny ledge with both feet.

"Allison, call her over." She yelled into the forced wind.

Allison, half over the precipice and feet dangling over the cliff with the weight of her gut in the ground, leaned over to one side.

"Over here, you ridiculous hag!"

The woman turned, never just her head. It was always her whole body and head, and she was quick. Sarah swung without thinking – she had no time to. The same green flash sprang out from the gemstone, same as it did in the witch's hut. Sarah saw a cut layer of fabric and a fall. The white body disappeared except for a hoop of garment at her eye level.

She stayed, and she listened. Her breath was visible by the loose dirt from the overhanging in front of her, her eyes peered just over the edge until her nerves strengthened. She pulled herself up and Allison fell in behind her. A white circle of cut garment laid on the ground; in the center, were a pair of ankles and feet.

"She's crawling toward Mary, Sarah get'er." They ran past the trail of blood and stood over the crawling woman. Its eyes were sheet white. Sarah looked down at her and began to slash, first at her leg's, which peeled from off her body like meat slices, but the woman still crawled.

Again, she slashed; the green glares reigned down from over her shoulder but still the woman crawled, getting closer and closer to the edge.

Finally, though only head, neck, and shoulder and arm were left attached; she still tried at grasping dirt and grass and the left side of her face was pressed to the ground.

The moon shined down on the cut-up body of Allison's monster. The one who looked their own age. One who could've been a friend of theirs, a friend had she not been cursed, or a demon, or used, or whatever. The monster whose face showed pain, agony, sorrow and...tears. Sarah's heart ached, her hand shakily went up high above her -and with tears running down her cheeks- it fell with the final blow. Blood and cleanly cut body parts lay all around the girls and over the clearing of blood-stained grass.

Allison and Sarah reached over the edge of the cliff and stretched down the rocks to grab Mary Gene, pulling her up. The three laid there, at the top, looking at the stars and the moon, feeling the cool breeze across their face as they caught their breath. Sarah reached over and pulled the lantern up to herself not daring to look around.

Chapter 7

The path brought them inland away from the cliffs of the sea. It didn't have to be lined in the white-orange tips of iron sticks (even though it was) because the natural landscape funneled them with the head-high rock formations between the sea and them, and to the right, brush and briers that closely hugged the black curtain that stood higher than the tallest trees; that curtain to which no light came in or out.

They began to descend a long hill that gave way to a valley. A whisper of fog receded, revealing a short clearing pressed against a line of tall trees, like sentinels.

The sentinels were some of the tallest trees that Sarah had ever seen. They stood like soldiers, guardians of the forest, their trunks were big and straight, spaced evenly apart. They had no limbs or leaves until the very tops which sat like helmets, -pine tree canopies. They reflected the white armor of moonlight, and they held back the jet-black shadows of earth behind them.

"Beautiful." Sarah said unconsciously.

"Dangerous"

Three screams came out in unison. Ava came from out of the bushes with arms straight out, palms pushing down and eyes wide open.

"Would you all, keep it down!" She said, in a low earnest tone.

"Oh Ava, it's you." Allison said with her hand still covering her heart. "Allison. Mary..? How did you make it out here?!"

"That's how." Mary Gene pointed down at Sarah's left hand. Ava looked down, at the blood-dripping necklace with its faint glowing emerald.

"You have a weapon?"

"And it cuts like butter." Allison added. Ava rubbed her hands together. "Oh, this is going to be fun then." And she then did something very few people get to see from her –short joyful hops.

"Maybe we can finally be free of Midnight." She smiled, "Oh, I would love to be free again, and maybe I will haunt a ship, and be out again in the open seas." Ava, with eyes closed, raised her face into the sky; the breeze brushed her hair back. Sarah felt, at that moment, she was not on this island.

"Who's Midnight?" Sarah asked, pulling Ava back to earth.

"Who's Midnight? They haven't told you?" Sarah shook her head. "You know her as Mara, but here she's known only as Midnight, and she is very prideful about that name too, she loves it...but hey, we need to do this..." Ava pointed, "here comes Midnight's black barrier."

They neared the edge of the woods. The curtain stopped a few feet back and moonlight attempted to penetrate the trees before them, most of its light fading before it reached the ground.

Ava picked up a branch. "Grab something to protect yourself with." Allison and Mary Gene went out into the bushes and Allison came back with a large rock; Mary held two sharp sticks.

Ava was about to speak again, but just then a howl came from the belly of the hollows, echoing up, winding around the trees. They looked down into the forest. Into the black chaos of trees and bushes, and all of the hideaways a wolf could wait for them.

Sarah knuckles whitened up around the chain after the howl switched to blood thirsting grunts and panting; it moved in the darkness, never in the same place twice, getting closer at each pass.

The girls huddled up one to another, that is except for Ava, who stood out in front two paces. Sarah looked down at this girl's hands that were visibly shaking, but still Ava's sharp eyes kept track of each pant, and each grunt; she followed something beyond the trees adjusting left and again back to the right, when suddenly it all fell silent.

The sound, the only sound, was that of breaths and of their shuffling feet. Ava's hand tightened over the branch; her searching had stopped. She stared at one spot that was very close to them. It was near, right around where some bushes were tucked close to trees and were heavy in shadow.

She moved with a step, one, then two, Sarah and the others close behind her, but then Sarah blinked and there it was, midair coming straight up at them. White teeth, shining claws and brown eyes landed on Ava in a fury of black fur.

Ava, on her back held the large stick, backed into the wolf's mouth. It frantically whipped its head from side to side, but Ava moved counter to it with gritty determination. It was slobbering and foaming at the mouth, dripping all around in the fight. Sarah spun her necklace faster and faster until she was right up to it, and just at the moment it felt good to strike, the wolf jumped back for a new approach causing her to miss. Ava yelled in surprise and swung her branch wildly at her feet. The wolf had latched down to her boot and was gnawing and tugging on her, pulling her in jerks, like it was trying to rip the foot from her leg. The branch came down at its closed eyes and ricocheted of its snout and head. It seemed to only get madder.

Sarah could only react; she took the wolf's ear in her right-hand twisting and pulling it with her whole strength as she might do in tug-a-war. The wolf let out a yelp, and its eyes turned sharp red, like stained glass. It tried to swing away but Sarah gripped tighter. It turned to bite her, but her left hand reflexed out, which the wolf readily took in its mouth and Sarah seeing smoke forming immediately, shoved her hand further down its throat and let go of the necklace. Her face set in involuntary disgust, as she ripped her hand back out.

The wolf's eyes changed into a sudden surprise, and it began to thrashed about, trying to escape from the pain, but it was of no avail. Only three moves into its *dance of agony*, it stumbled to its side heaving for breath and twitched its legs like it was still running. It attempted to cry but couldn't. They watched from a distance as the twitching got weaker and weaker, holding their weapons over their heads until finally it laid there stiff.

The smoke from its mouth past the limp tongue, and it sizzled and smoked around the fur from underneath.

They stood over the body of the black wolf.

"Help me flip him over." Ava said. They all bent over and grabbed a leg. Its lifeless body rolled to their will. Underneath it, sitting in a pool of blood and fur was Sarah's necklace. Ava, carefully went to her knees over the wolf's body and she began to pet it a few times, from the shoulders down to its tail. At the final pass she let her hands rest on its shoulders.

"Help me up, please." She said without looking. Holding the arms of her friends, she looked up at the trees. "It really is pretty out here, isn't it?"

"Yes," Sarah replied. "...are you glad to be rid of your wolf, Ava?"

"Yeah..." she said looking back at it, "but I would be even happier if I could get its pelt."

Chapter 8

The floor was covered in orange and brown leaves and pine needles. Their eyes adjusted and rays came at angles to the needle covered ground. They walked in the soft shadows of the giants, in the peaceful air from calm seas, and in the hope of a broken curse – in the shape of a necklace.

It wasn't too much longer when they came into the lowest point of the valley, where clear and solid grounds between the tall trees gave way to black and stinking swampland where the short gnarly trees grew. No light made it down here. The muddy waters were as black as ink in a vile. There were large round rocks that came up just above the crest of its smooth flat surface, giving a footing and path through the swamp. Even with the glow of the lantern they could only see one or two rocks ahead, each one large enough for only three girls to stand on.

Sarah and Ava went first while Allison and Mary stayed one boulder back. After a few moments of jumping from rock to rock their surroundings were ingulfed by darkness. The light of the lantern just barely reaching to their next jump. Sarah could no longer see skies or moon, only black. So carefully they made their way through the swamp from rock to rock in a slow careful pace.

Sarah leaped over to her next stone but stopped.

"Ava." She tried to say, her heart beating louder than her words. Ava had the lantern, but Sarah saw something.

"Ava!" She managed a little louder. "There's hair. Like just hanging down from the tree."

"Hair? Oh crap, is it blonde hair?" Ava jumped over to Sarah.

"Yes. Ava it's hanging straight down." Ava shuffled around her.

"Oh my God." Ava gasped. Sarah's hands covered her mouth and she, without warning began to cry.

"What's wrong?" Allison cried from behind.

"It's Kailey!" Ava cried. She leaned over to the tree from the rock and desperately pulled at the twisting limbs that had been tangled around Kailey's upside-down body and covered her mostly up. Ava pulled and clawed at it like a dog escaping from its cage. Tears covered her face, she could not get anywhere with it, even the small branches refused to break off, only twisting back to their spots. Kailey's chest was laboring in a small space between some branches.

Sarah gained some of herself back and began digging at the branches with Ava, but she had no success. She suddenly remembered her necklace though and pushed herself back upright to use it. She swung at the branch at the side of Kailey's body, and with a gyre of light it cut the branch which bled a syrup from its wound.

Allison jumped over. Sarah slashed and slashed and Ava threw each branch off to the sides. They came to the last branch that looked like a large five-pronged claw that covered her face, neck, and shoulders. Ava and Allison with one hand on the tree and the other under Kailey's shoulders waited for Sarah's last few strikes.

Sarah swung at the last branch peeling it away and Kailey's body fell into the arms of her friends. They, with difficulty, pulled her up over to the rock, and Allison, losing her balance, jumped back to where Mary Gene was watching intently.

Her face was blood red, and Ava kneeled over her, lightly slapping at her face. Sarah's hand was on her chest, and she felt the rhythm of her heartbeat and her lungs filling and deflating. Kailey was waking up with short intervals of consciousness.

After they massaged and rubbed her limbs for several minutes she came to, and in one last look of daze and confusion, and seeing Ava over her with a relieved expression, she managed a smile, softly lifting her hand, caressing at Ava's cheek.

"How?" She asked weakly.

"It's because of Sarah, but nevermind that now. Let's get you up."

They lifted her up and Sarah held her steady for a minute. Kailey was stable though weak and she stretched a bit, straightening her dress, and let the blood flow out to the rest of her body, but they had no more time. They had to keep moving -and they did.

Ava jumped first, then Sarah. Kailey jumped, but landed wrong, she began falling backwards swinging her arms trying to catch balance. Sarah threw her arms out and grabbed her pulling her back into what was essentially a group hug.

"Oh my god, Thank you." Kailey's breath returned to her. "Ava? How did you make it through?"

"You are about to find out, thanks to Sarah..." Sarah's cheeks began to blush.

"How?" Kailey's face still washed in confusion. Ava placed her hand on her shoulder.

"Kailey..." She said more softly than Sarah had heard her speak, "What happens to you here will never happen again. Do you trust me." Kailey stared into Ava's eyes and smiled.

"Ok. I believe you."

THEY HAD GOTTEN TO a place where they could see faintly a field in between the limbs of the low and twisted trees. They are the barrier of the swamplands. The mud seemed shallower here. They kept jumping from rock to rock, but a yell broke the silence behind Sarah. Everyone looked back quickly.

Allison had fallen and splashed into the nasty swamp mud – her lantern lost in the inked-black waters.

Sarah hollered toward where she last saw the light. "Allison! Allison are you alright?"

"EEWWUKK!" she heard through the dark. She heard the slapping of wet clothes on a hard surface. Slap, Slap, Slap -Allison climbed back onto her rock.

"Yes..." Sarah heard, "...I'm alright."

They leaped to each new rock in the dark, landing as a cat would, scraping knees and palms, in time, finally making it to her. The top layer of mud on her body already begun to dry. Her face grimaced when she moved to wipe the large clumps of dirt off, but when she was gritting in disgust, she suddenly smiled and laughed, and they all laughed -echoing in the low dark swamp.

"I simply can't wait for this to be over." She finally said.

THE GRASS CAME IN VIEW through a set of twisted black locust trees. It came to just one last row.

Sarah looked at Kailey who stood there hugging herself, rubbing up and down her arms.

"I hope you never go through something like that again." Sarah said looking intently at her. Kailey, with a sudden move, embraced her and held her very tightly.

"We won't have to if you can get past Midnight." She whispered.

"Isn't that the place?" Mary Gene cried. She gestured to a building way over all the pasture type fields. Ava looked to where Mary was pointing.

"That's it." She started to walk up toward it. Allison grabbed her by her clothes and pulled her back.

"Wait."

"What's wrong?" Ava said looking shocked.

"I have a question for you ladies." They gathered around her, "Do you think that Midnight knows we are still alive?"

Chapter 9

Sarah, walking alone, saw in the far distance over clear rolling hills a building that looked the shape of an old country church without a steeple. While she walked, large shadows from slow moving clouds came from the church, moving across the fields in intervals, and under and behind her to unknown places past the sea. She secretly enjoyed watching them while she traveled closer and closer to her strange antagonist.

Soon she was pressing up the final hill, a small worn path led up to the building. One solitary tree stood in front, off to the left, and when she made it up to that tree, she was awestruck. The building was not a building at all, and it was not small, they were trees.

Trees formed at either side and made up the walls. They bowed to each other making an apex roof... as if to be silent witnesses of all things that happened here and that will happen.

It was bigger than she had imagined it – kin to a great cathedral. Little sprouted trees filled in the gaps, keeping her from seeing inside; so, she aligned herself to the front opening and held tightly to emerald, chain and all.

Just before stepping into the threshold, a cold breeze blew pushing her hood and clothes tight against the back of her body, as if it were beckoning her in. She walked slow, down the center of the great open hall letting time for her eyes to adjust to the darkness. When suddenly, she realized that near the end of it all, stood a girl. She could only make out the parts where moonlight touches her, for a dark shadow cut from her left shoulder to right hip, shrouding neck, face, and eyes.

She shuffled, hesitantly, a little closer but stopped and perceived the girl's head moving slightly up, looking her in the eye.

"I see you made it – unscathed..." She let out a short giggle. "I mean relatively." Her body was as still as a statue.

"You see, I told them not to hurt you..." Again, a mocking giggle, "...physically I mean."

"I only wanted them to Rip Your Ugly Heart Out!" Sarah skin jumped; the echo resounded off the walls...

Her voice went seamlessly back to even.

"How did you like seeing your friends suffer? ...How did you like seeing them in pain, and in blood...and death!" The words echoed all around Sarah taunting her and she remembers Mary's face being slapped and bleeding, and the grotesque way in which she punished Kailey.

"Why are you doing this to me?... To us?"

"I'm afforded this privilege, you see..." Sarah sensed a smile. "...when I come across girls like you." She amused herself so much at this, Sarah imagined her bursting apart, like a doll at the seams.

"You ghoul. How do you live with yourself?" Midnight burst into insane laughter. She was bent toward Sarah and her straight brown hair dipped slightly in the moonlight, vibrating at the force of heaving lungs full of scorn.

She again made herself erect.

"That's funny coming from you." Midnights body became rigid again.

"You are the reason you are here." Sarah could hear her teeth gritting now. Midnight's breath seemed as if it were at the first stages of seething.

"You selfish soul... You weak minded...Your ugly and deceitful heart– that you've buried – and the stories and the excuses you tell yourself Night After Night!"

Anger resounded through the darkness.

"You wouldn't be able to see it if you dug for it the rest of your LIFE!" Her words beat against the walls and reached the ceiling where it scattered the hidden black birds into the night sky. Leaves and feathers floated to the cathedral floor.

The new light that came didn't show Midnight's face but did reveal a large round pit in the back center of the hall. Sarah trembled at the sudden rage and the pounding of the wings; she stood there shaking with her arms crossed in a hug.

"You don't know anything about me?" She said in a weak – almost inner voice.

"Oh no..." Midnight stepped out from the shadow. Sarah gasped, with eyes wide, for she stood at arm's length from a twisted twin of her-own-self. She had brown hair, but Sarah's, blonde. She had brown eyes that glimmered at times red but Sarah's, emerald green. Midnight's face made an expression so ugly and full of rage.

"You both can go to HELL!" She screamed at Sarah. Sarah's blood ran cold to shiver. Her stomach turned and twisted, dizzying, drained to weakness. Her body fell limp to the dirty hard ground. She saw the bare weavings of the roof's limbs. Her dizziness swirled to her eyes like if she opened them just below water's surface.

SHE SAW HER MOTHER standing at their open front door. She was arrayed elegantly in a black and gold dress, her father besides, in suit and tie. They were beaming with smiles up the stairs at her, but she felt rage in the body she now pseudo-possessed.

"Why can't I go to my friends?" Sarah heard herself say, trying only little to conceal all the rage. Their faces turned, from smiles.

"We told you...It's something we can't plan for you to do last second, honey."

"I don't care. I can call her. She'll let me come over right now!" She said trying less to conceal it.

"No." Her father said. "It's your mother's big night, please don't ruin it."

"YOU'RE the one ruining it, I have to stay here – alone – while you get to go out and have fun, HOW IS THAT FAIR!" The fierceness echoed throughout the halls. Her father wasn't smiling now.

"That's enough! Now wish your mother good luck."

Sarah felt herself crying, begging, pleading for herself, now, to stop.

"NO." She stomped on the top step. Her parents turned and were closing the door behind. She saw nothing but red.

"YOU BOTH CAN GO TO HELL!" She screamed as loudly as she could. When the door opens – fear swallowed her body like an ocean. She heard through the door, the crying of her mother.

Her father's face was blood red.

"You never talk to your mother that way again..." His teeth gritting. "Get to your room now." In response – A stomp. Suddenly, a raging face started to barrel up the stairs. She turned and ran to the dark room – her heart pounding -even Sarah's also-, tears wanted to fall, they wanted to come endlessly, now, but they wouldn't -not in the vision.

"WORDS ARE A POWERFUL thing, yes?" Midnight said pleasantly. Sarah, again, was sitting on the hard ground of an empty cathedral. Bawling unashamedly – she didn't take her hands from the dirt to wipe them away.

Again, a sound of her 'own voice' came.

"You see how well you upset them. Oh, what a wonderful lather you had them in." -Eyes closed; Sarah's head shook in her crying.

"I couldn't have done it better myself. The great anger, the speed, the rain and the wind, the mountain road. You couldn't have planned it better the way you killed your parents, BRAVO! BRAVO!" Midnight clapped to emphasis the bravado in the 'cathedral' – its taunting echo...

Sarah's face stricken in horror, stared up at her. The clapping persisted and Sarah's face turn red.

"It wasn't my fault! Anything could've happened..." her eyes began darting left and right, "A deer could've..."

"...Could have run out into the road. Another driver could've had their high beams on..." Midnight kept on in mocking tones, "...the car could've lost traction. I've heard it all before."

Midnight abruptly stopped, her body snapped at attention, her head went back, and she looked straight up at the moon. She looked down again with big toothy smile.

> "Well. It's time. I hear the pit calling..." *That hideous giggle again* "...calling for a murderer."

Sarah had no intention to get up, she would fight savagely right there, but, behind Midnight, in the dark corners of the cathedral and near the pit, she saw her friends.

Midnight turned and started walking away.

When Midnight neared the pit, she stopped. Sarah's heart beat loudly.

Midnight bent down in front of it. It was near the direction where she saw one of the girls, but everything lied still. The sound of something sliding filled in echoes. Sarah felt her breath catch. Midnight turned back around and came with her book in hand. To the front of the pit.

It's time. Sarah thought to herself. Midnight opened the book and began to chant. Sarah new this was her last chance.

"STOP!" Sarah was ignored – Midnight was still chanting.

"STOP I SAID." Midnight's head never raised as if Sarah were no more important than if she were a fly.

"Who gives you the authority to do this?" She asked with as much air of importance as she could muster. Midnight gestures the book up slightly, signifying that that was it – not breaking her rhythm.

Panic set in. "Why are you keeping the others."

Midnight alluded to nothing, and the winds shifted outside the cathedral. The leaves fell and black feathers were carried in by cool sea airs.

"Where did you come from…" Her brain searching for anything until… "When's your judgement coming?"

Midnight's head twitched to one side, but still the chants. A dull lifeless glow of red started to show at the sunken walls of the pit. Sarah was tossing between panic and anger; she suddenly struck on an idea. Grabbing tighter her emerald.

"What is your name?" She asked with authority. Midnight stops and folds the book over her fore finger. Her head raised; each iris glowed red like stained glass. An amused smile creeped across her face.

"My name is Midn…" A tackle, they pinned her to the ground quickly. Each girl maneuvered over her -Kailey and Allison had her left arm, Ava the right and Mary bear-hugged her legs together, using her whole body like a clamp. Sarah saw the book tumble and slide to the edge of the pit.

The surprised look on Midnight's face was strange to Sarah – it didn't fit somehow, but it lasted only a breath, when it turned with a fury, into rage.

"You little BASTA…"

"Sarah. The emerald!" Ava cried. Sarah leaped over top of Midnight's thrashing body, landing on her like a mirror; Sarah used her thumb to push the emerald down on her forehead with all of her might, as if trying to cave it in. The green light coursed through veins and cracked past slivers of red iris until Midnight screamed and her eyes died away in muddy brown pools of color.

Sarah felt a strange sensation and before she could get off her, she fell through ash and clothes, to the solid ground beneath. Mary points in panic. "Sarah the book!", and as panic leads to panic, she dived at it and when she laid hold of it the edge of the loose dirt gave way and dumped her in the black pit.

"Use the emerald!" Said one.

"Through the book," Cried another.

She obliged their demands, as quick as a fighter hearing his corner. With emerald first, she went into the book hands, face, and all.

Chapter 10

Black rolls of clouds internalized by lightning and thunder flashed by her so fast that she hardly registered them at all. Then, it went black, and a sudden thump jolted her.

She opened her eyes and found that she was sitting in her spot in the bookstore – alone. Her eyes gathered its senses, and she saw the grandfather clock in the corner -three minutes after midnight.

Her guts churned up something past her throat. Her hands came up to her mouth just in time to catch blood mixed in syrupy black licorice. The black syrup lay in the blood, like veins, and at that very moment headlights danced through the windows and off the walls.

Sarah got up and quickly ran to the kitchen, washing off her hands and her face. She looked at her reflection in the kitchen's window frantic and hurried out in time to meet her grandfather in the cafe.

"Hey girl, where's the fire?" He smiled with his hands on her shoulders. He looked around.

"Did you have fun tonight?" He gently started toward the kitchen. Sarah stayed in front of him nervously, worried that she might have missed some blood. She scanned it, seeing only empty cups and plates and little spills here and there.

He put his keys in the bowl by the fridge, turned the light off as he left. Halfway through the dark café, she grabbed his arm to stop him.

"Grandpa, won't you stay up with me a little longer?" Her heart earnestly poured into her words. He sensed its importance immediately and nodded. She, holding his arm, guided him to the main room. He stopped to blow out some candles.

"Where are all of your friends?" He asked.

"They... They're home." She said stifling her tears back. She drew him down with her to her spot –seeing the closed books of her friends.

He sat with his legs laid straight out, she put a pillow on his lap, and he unwrapped a sucker to eat it, and it *seemed* he didn't have a care in the world -looking at his books. She looked up at him, in envy, and she could have stayed there too, for hours and hours, and days and days.

She asked him of all the stories he had read about, the ones where people cheated death. She asked him about all the ways people mourned in times past, and in other cultures. She especially asked how her mother was growing up and about all the mean things that she said and did to him, when she was a child.

Her grandfather answered everything with patience and sympathy. He told of all the stories that she wouldn't hear from her mother or her father. He spoke well and in comfort, and just before she would fall asleep –she would confess to him.

And just maybe, in this now sacred room, and surrounded by the ancients, she could heal.